RULES OF SUMMER

Shaun Tan

LOTHIAN
Children's Books

This is what I learned last summer:

Never leave a red sock on the clothesline.

Never eat the last olive at a party.

Never drop your jar.

Never leave the back door open overnight.

Never step on a snail.

WALL - 150 below
water level

shallow

Never be late for a parade.

5300

45°

5300

Never ruin a perfect plan.

Never argue with an umpire.

Never give your keys to a stranger.

Never forget the password.

Never ask for a reason.

Never lose a fight.

Never wait for an apology.

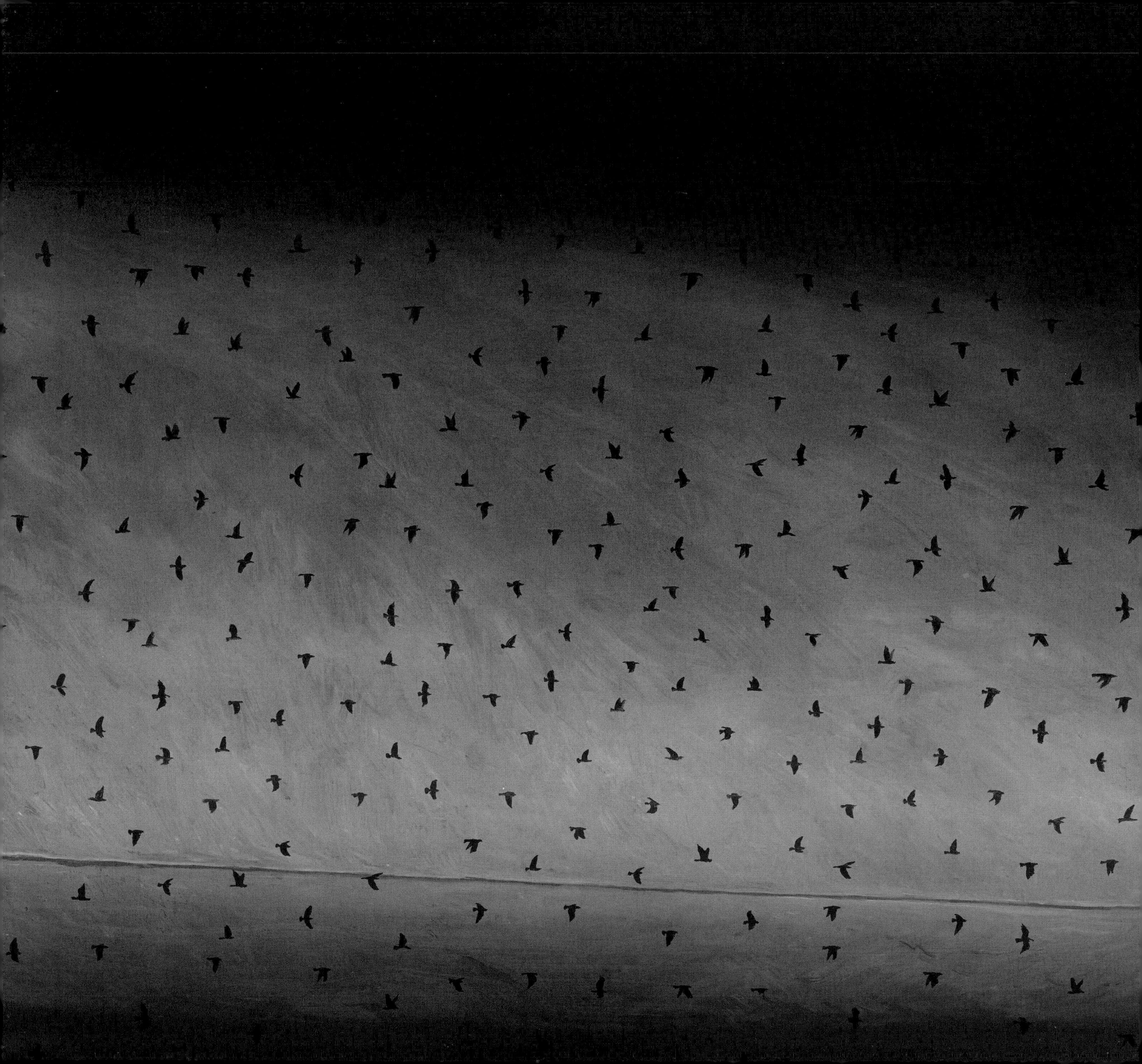

Always bring bolt cutters.

Always know the way home.

Never miss the last day of summer.

That's it.